You're a hen!

ISBN 978-94-026-0054-4
This book is also available as e-book: ISBN 978-94-026-0056-8

Cover design and layout: Teo van Gerwen
Translation: Marion Coonen-Singor

www.jacquesvriens.nl
www.henkkneepkens.nl
www.aerialmediacom.nl
www.facebook.com/Aerialmediacompany

Aerial Media Company bv.
Postbus 6088
4000 HB Tiel, The Netherlands

Jacques Vriens and Henk Kneepkens

You're a hen!

Aerial Media Company

100 chickens

Tim is out on his bike when he sees something white
by the roadside.
"Hey," he says. "There's a dead hen."
He strokes her soft little head gently.
Suddenly, the hen opens her eyes and says, "Burp!"
"Oh, so you're still alive," laughs Tim. "But only just."

“Don’t worry, hen,” he whispers.
“I’ll take you home to our
henhouse to get better.”

He lifts her carefully onto his bike.
The hen does nothing, until he
rides over a bump in the road.
Then she says, “Burp!”

Tim proudly carries the hen into his house.
“I’ve saved a hen!” he calls out.
The family gathers round.
“Hmm, it’s a bit of an excuse for a hen,” says mum.
“It’s practically dead,” says dad.
“Get it in the pan for dinner,” says big brother.
“No!” shouts Tim. “She’s my hen.”
“Burp!” says the hen.
Big brother laughs. “You can’t call that a hen – it doesn’t even know it is a hen anymore. We’re having chicken for tea tonight.”
But Tim runs away as fast as he can. With his hen.

Tim puts his hen down, looks her in the eye and explains gently, “You’re a hen.”
“Burp!” says the hen.
“You’re a hen!” says Tim.
“Burp!” says the hen.

“You’re not ending up as dinner,” says Tim. “I’m taking you to the vet.”

“Can she walk?”
says the vet.
“No.”
“Can she fly?”
“No.”
“Can she at least
cluck?”

“Burp!”
says the hen.
The vet slowly
shakes his head.
“I’m sorry. She was
a nice hen once,
but there’s nothing
else I can do.”

"Right, this is a henhouse," explains Tim.

"Because remember, you're a hen."

The hens in the henhouse come over to have a look.

"Burp!" says Tim's hen.

The other hens don't like it. They start to cluck and peck at Tim and his hen.

"Go away, you stupid birds!" shouts Tim, flapping his arms.

But they just cluck and peck harder.

Tim stands up and picks up his hen.

"Come on you – we're leaving!" he mutters, and storms off.

“Somehow you’ll have to become a normal hen again,” says Tim. “Otherwise you’ll end up in the frying pan or be clucked and pecked out of the henhouse. I’ll just have to give you hen lessons.”

“Now, pay attention, hen. This is where your egg comes out, see?”
Tim pokes his finger under her tail feathers.
“Come on, it’s easy! Just go ‘cluck, cluck, cluck’ and concentrate on making an egg. It’ll all come back to you if you try.”
Tim waits. The hen eyes him beadily.
“Burp!” says the hen. .

“Right, here comes lesson two,” says Tim. “This is important – it’s the cluck lesson. Listen and repeat after me: cluck, cluck, cluck!”

“Burp, burp, buuuurrppp!” says the hen.

"Hen, you have to try HARDER. Don't you get it? You're a hen! YOU'RE A HEN!!" bellows Tim.
The hen says nothing – not even, "Burp!"
"Okay, lesson three," sighs Tim. "This is your flying lesson. Surely this will bring it all back?"

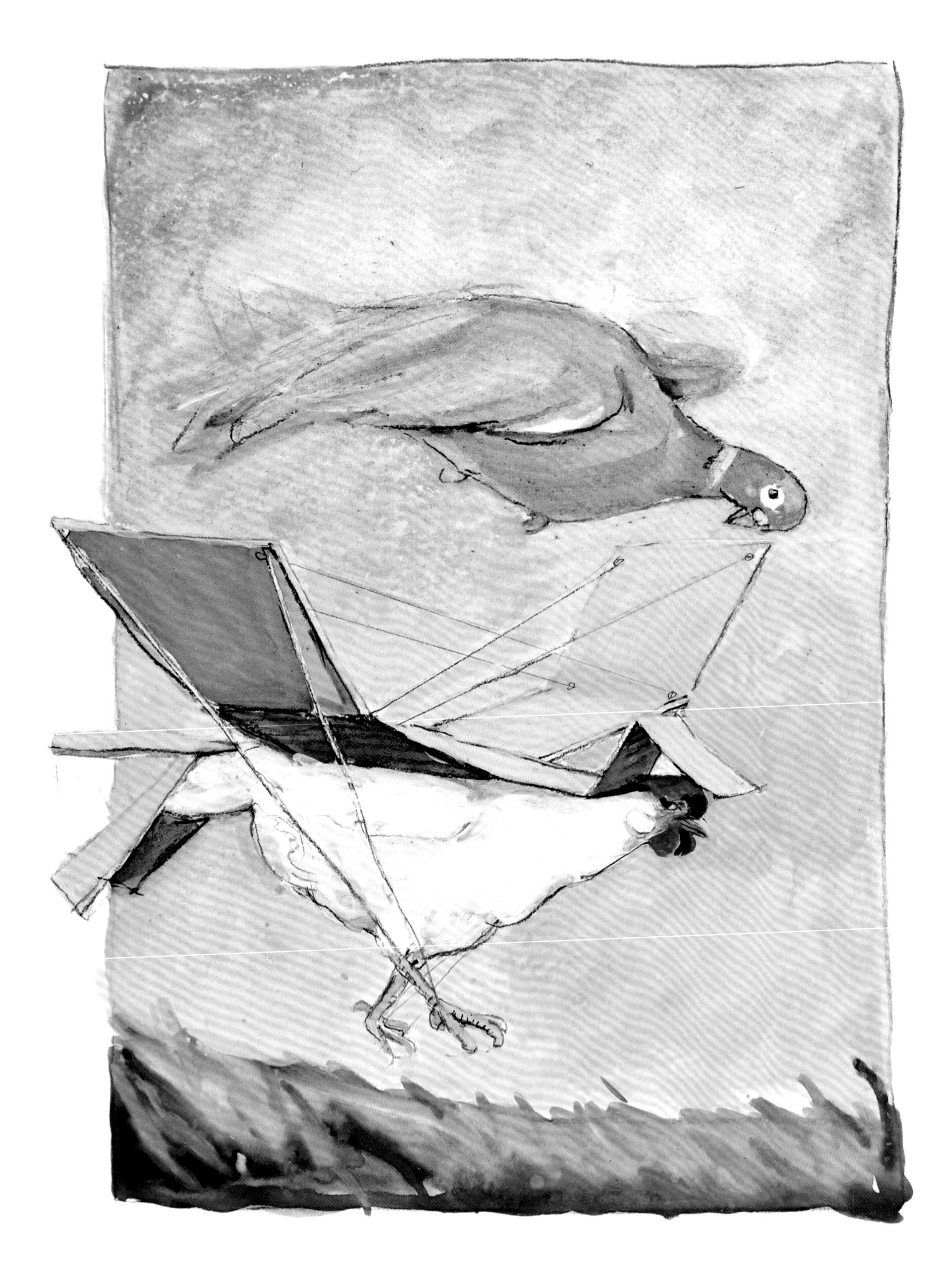

Tim flaps his arms to show the hen how to fly. Nothing happens.

"You might be a hen, but you're not much of a hen," Tim admits finally.

"Hang on," he says. "Do you even want to be a hen?"

"Burp!" says the hen.

"Because maybe you could be a duck or a parrot instead!"

"Burp!"

"Okay, a duck then," says Tim. "I'll help you be a duck. You just need duck lessons. Lesson one is the swimming lesson. Pay attention, duck."

But however much Tim splashes about in a puddle, the ‘duck’ won’t swim.
“Okay, you’re not a duck either, so let’s try you as a parrot,” says Tim, painting the hen with beautiful colours. “Now you’re a beautiful parrot with all the colours of the rainbow on your feathers.”

The hen struts about looking very fine, but then it begins to rain.

“Oh no, you useless hen!” gasps Tim. “Look at all your colours running in the rain. Now you’re just an ordinary hen again.”

"I'm just about out of ideas, hen," sighs Tim. "I don't know what sort of bird you are. You can't lay eggs or cluck or fly, you can't swim and you can't keep your bright colours. You don't seem to be able to do anything."
He kicks the ground. "But I won't let them eat you! I'll find you a place to hide – come on!"

Suddenly there's a sound from behind the bushes.

"Cock-a-doodle-doo!"

And again, "Cock-a-doodle-doooooo!"

The hen lifts her head, blinks and says…

"…cluck!"

"What did you say, hen?" gasps Tim.

"Cluck!"

"Woo hoo, you ARE a hen!" shouts Tim, jumping up and down.

"Cluck!" says the hen. "Cluck, cluck, CLUCK!"

Tim and the two birds walk happily to the henhouse.
“You ARE a hen – I knew you were!” sings Tim.
“Cock-a-doodle-doo!” crows the cockerel.
“Cluck!” clucks the hen.
“You just needed to be with your old friend the cockerel didn’t you?” says Tim. “Now everything will be all right!”
“Cock-a-doodle-CLUCK!” agree the cockerel and hen together.

We used to have hens at home in a large loft with a run.

There was one tame hen.

Many years later when I was out on my bike, a white hen got caught between my wheels.

The bird ran confused onto the motorway and you can probably guess what happened.

Since then I've never forgotten that hen. I started to make more and more drawings of it.

When I showed them to Jacques Vriens he got so enthusiastic, he immediately wrote a story.

So you see a picture book can get started in many different ways.

Henk Kneepkens